UNHEALED *Hearts* MAKE UNHEALTHY *Choices*

LIVING BEYOND SEXUAL ADDICTION

REBECCA P. WOOD

ISBN 979-8-89112-056-3 (Paperback)
ISBN 979-8-89112-057-0 (Digital)

Covenant Books
11661 Hwy 707
Murrells Inlet, SC 29576
www.covenantbooks.com

As Shirley Thomas shared "Your Life in Book Form" at the Women of Virtue Conference hosted by Benji Clark Mallory, God reminded me that He had already given me the book titled *Unhealed Hearts Make Unhealthy Choices*. Having worked on it in bits and pieces in the past twenty-three years, now that I am free from other ministry responsibilities, it is time to get it done.

April 1, 2022

Contents

Chapter 1

INSTABILITY AND
LESSONS NOT LEARNED

My earliest memory is waiting for my parents to bring home my third little brother. I was not quite four years old. My daddy had already been transferred three times, and we had moved from my birthplace in Florida to Tennessee, and now to Georgia. The next memory is chasing my oldest brother, sticking out my foot, and tripping him. His forehead hit the corner of the door casing and he was rushed to the emergency room. I remember hiding in the laundry room, trying to avoid trouble.

Hiding when we sin is as old as time.[1] Even at four years old, the laws written in my heart told me it was wrong to trip my brother, but my foolishness told me it would be fun to see what happened.[2]

Every moment of every day, we make choices; most of them are unconscious decisions based on our upbringing, circumstances, and desires at the moment.[3] We choose what we will wear, where we will go, what we will eat, and who we will associate with. But we also choose whether we will respond to outward stimuli or react to them. Failure to deliberately choose to respond means circumstances will cause us to react, and that is rarely the best choice.

Every choice carries consequences based on natural law.[4] We throw something up, and gravity will pull it down. We lash out in anger and then regret the hurt it causes and the time it takes to

1

rebuild trust. When we plant seeds of discord, we will reap a harvest of confusion and disrespect.

Moving to North Carolina at age five, I grew up in a small town with multifamily barbecues, football games in the vacant lot, and sledding the West Kivett Street hill. I had opportunities to form friendships. Daddy was handsome, funny, and always the life of the party. He became my hero. Because he traveled during the week, I looked forward to weekends when he was home. Mom was always there, but I was jealous of the attention Daddy gave her. I dreamed of marrying him one day.

Each year, we made one or two trips to visit Mom's mother in Dublin, Georgia, where my uncle and his wife took care of her. Another uncle lived nearby, and an aunt was just an hour away, so there were at least fifteen first cousins when we congregated at Christmas.

During the summer visits, when distant relatives often joined us, an army of children and adults invaded the house, covering the porches and spilling out into the yard. We played in the corncrib or the hayloft, where we loved to see who was brave enough to jump.

Bedridden with arthritis, my grandmother was confined to her room. This left us free to use her old wooden wheelchair for a racecar, seeing how fast we could push one another around the porches.

With unpainted lap siding, beaded heart pine tongue and groove lumber throughout, wrap-around porches, and kitchen and dining room separated from the main house by a "dogtrot," the old house remained much like it was when she and my grandfather purchased the farm in 1919. It still had a functional outhouse and well, from which water was drawn regularly. In the summertime, we bathed in a washtub on the back porch until indoor plumbing was installed after my grandmother's death in 1958.

On one of these semiannual visits when I was five or six, we thought my daddy drowned in a boating accident on the river that runs between Dublin and East Dublin, Georgia. I remember going to the bank of the Oconee River and seeing my daddy's red and white Dodge station wagon parked there, and police were everywhere.

They found his overturned boat, and a massive search was launched to no avail.

It was a grueling time for everyone as Mom, my brothers, and I piled in with cousins, waiting until his death could be confirmed. Investigators and sympathetic neighbors came from every direction.

The only conversation I remember during this time was an insurance investigator asking mom, "Did he have 'Cat Paw' heels?" They had found a footprint that had those heels leading from the water to the road. It was Mom's youngest brother who finally found my daddy living in Texas with another woman. My uncle convinced him to return.

Once reunited, we headed back to our home in North Carolina. Nervous breakdown did not mean much to me, except that Mom went to work and Annie came to help around the house. We were more careful not to upset Daddy, and we ate a lot of dried beans and corn bread. Otherwise, life was pretty much as it had been, at least on the surface. At first, I did not recognize the changes in Daddy. But soon, his mood swings and violent behavior made me want to get away. The anchor I clung to was no longer safe, and as a child, I did not know how to find the true Anchor.

We continued riding bikes, going to school, playing in the creek, and sledding in the winter. Not being very coordinated, I was usually the last to be chosen for teams. Add to that red hair, freckles, and glasses, and the jokes never ended at my expense. I was a gangly little girl growing into an awkward adolescent.

My hero's image had been tarnished when he faked his own death, which caused me more confusion than the thought of leaving my friends, the pet cemetery behind the garage, and everything familiar. The six years we lived in North Carolina would be the longest time I would spend in one place until I returned to Dublin at age forty-five.

A little girl loves her daddy and needs to be secure in his love. This is the best preparation for her to someday be a wife. Without a proper relationship with the parent of the opposite sex, many children suffer an identity crisis that hinders their developing healthy relationships in the future.

From the small town of Asheboro, North Carolina, to the suburbs of Dallas, Texas, was quite a change. Starting sixth grade in a much larger school was just one of the differences. I did not have any real friends that year, so when a young man asked me to sit by him when our class went to a Chinese restaurant as an exercise in culture, I was flattered and surprised. At twelve, he was my first boyfriend. Our romance was short-lived when we moved again that summer.

Once again, I was a newcomer, this time, entering junior high. Rather than learn how to work through difficulties with my classmates, I looked forward to moving to Northwest Texas when the school year ended.

It was in Amarillo, in a big, new, two-story house, that my childhood was shattered when Daddy came into my room late one night, smelling of alcohol, and had his way with me. I was not only so shamed and humiliated but also so hurt that he had betrayed me that I held that dark secret for twenty-three years untold. Everything hidden in the dark will fester and rot. Painful secrets and shame can quickly become toxic. It took away what little self-esteem I had remaining. I felt worthless, violated, and even guilty, wondering if I had somehow caused this abuse.

In a fit of rage shortly thereafter, Daddy beat Mom and threatened to kill all of us. The police hid Mom, my brothers, and me while searching for my daddy. They could only hold him for seventy-two hours without formal charges, which she was reluctant to press, but that was enough time for us to fill the car with all we could carry and head north. Mom was bound for Minneapolis, Minnesota, but could not find work there, so we turned back to Des Moines, Iowa, where she immediately went to work at *Look* magazine.

For two years, we stayed in hiding, sending and receiving mail via Kansas City, Kansas, while living in a two-bedroom, upstairs apartment near Drake University. Hot-to-cold weather and suburbs to inner cities only added to the chaos in my adolescent mind, and I bordered on being delinquent.

Hidden things manifest in unpleasant ways. But light dispels darkness, so if you have secret hurts or secret sins, don't let them steal your life and your joy. God loves you and is for you.[5] In fact, before the foundation of the world, He made the way for you to become all He created you to become.[6] If you come to the Father through faith in Jesus Christ, His Son, He will accept you into His own family and seal you with His Spirit.[7] You can change, but not by yourself. Christ in you is the agent of change and our only hope of glory!

Chapter 2

PUSHING THE LIMITS

When I was caught shoplifting suntan lotion at age fourteen, Mom came and picked me up. Her question cut me deeply when she asked, "Is this where all of those records and clothes came from?" Music was my passion, and all of my babysitting money was used to buy the latest 45s, which I then traded among friends for several less-popular ones. We shared clothes at random, too, and I was hurt that Mom believed they were stolen. My face must have given her the answer she wanted because she never questioned me again. Except for a few pens from work (and too often God's time and tithe), that ended my career as a thief.

Becky, Linda, Pam, Shelly, and Sue—we were six best friends. Though we were not allowed to date in junior high, we could go in groups of guys and girls. My first kiss was shared with Darrell. He was blond and cute, and Shelly liked him too. Because he kissed me, I thought that meant I was something special. After all, Shelley was the most beautiful of the group, with clear features and long brown hair. Fortunately, the sexual revolution had not hit the Midwest in 1965.

Comparing ourselves to others is a self-destructive choice. There will always be prettier, richer, and more popular people, just as there will always be those who are less so. This is equally true spiritually, mentally, physically, and socially. It is a trap to think of others as more gifted instead of trusting that we were uniquely created for a divine purpose.[8] As long as we focus on others or ourselves, we will never discover our destiny and walk in its fulfillment, which is found in Christ alone.

At fifteen, we returned to Georgia on the advice of relatives and moved into the home in which Mom had been born, the one that my grandparents had bought shortly after they married, and that was so full of memories. Daddy joined us and was his charming self, so our house was usually filled with friends and relatives.

From a Washington Irving junior high class of several hundred to Dexter School, where there were twelve grades under one roof, it was quite a change. Most of my classmates accepted me, but our friendships were not the same, and I never totally felt like I belonged. They had been friends since first grade or earlier, and often their parents were long-term friends before that!

As the new girl in a small rural school, I got a lot of attention from boys, and I loved it. It was not uncommon to go out with one on Friday, another on Saturday, and to church with another on Sunday! Often I was called a tease because I did not understand that kissing and petting would arouse things best kept for marriage. But I was feeding my self-esteem any way I could, trying hard to fill a void only God can fill. Fourteen students graduated with me in 1970.

I was so desperate for worth at age sixteen that when I missed a date with a senior who I had a *big* crush on, I took an entire bottle of pills, trying to kill myself. My parents rushed me an hour away to an uncle who was a doctor. That next week was gone from my memory, except that I opened my eyes one time in their guest room. A week later, I woke up in my own bed with lots of cousins and friends coming by.

Truth is truth, whether we accept it or not. There is One by Whom we are totally accepted.[9] He knows us better than anyone ever will, and He has good plans for us. His natural laws do not change based on what we want or believe them to be.

Men and women were created to complement one another and multiply.[10] When a man and woman spend time alone together, they will grow closer until eventually they become one. That is why it is so important to guard your heart. Allow your heart to be healed in

Christ, and He will lead you to fulfillment because He created you with unique gifts and good plans. You have a purpose!

Every girl wants to be beautiful and cherished so she can give herself completely to her love. When young girls have been cherished by their fathers, they do not feel the need to search for that love from boys and men. For those of us whose relationship with our dads was not healthy, we should look to our Father for that love and affirmation, but most often, we are unaware that He desires a relationship with us, to cherish us and affirm our loveliness. But He does! He is love.[11]

The choice to date as many boys who asked me out was a poor substitute for the love of God, but it temporarily gave me some sense of worth. Just before my seventeenth birthday, my daddy died after a brief battle with lung cancer. There were mixed emotions. A part of me was glad because I feared what he might do next, and the guilt those thoughts brought weighed heavy on my heart.

Discovering a newspaper article with my parents' engagement announcement caused even more confusion when I did the math and realized they were married less than six months before I was born. It was soon after this bit of news I knew I needed God to help me, and at seventeen, I turned to Jesus. There was no way I could get beyond my sin and rebellion, so I asked Jesus if He would forgive me. By truly being sorry for my sin and trusting that He could help me turn from my ways, I surrendered my life to His hands. I willingly walked that little church aisle in front of everyone to acknowledge my faith was now in Jesus Christ.[12]

Though it seemed that nothing magical happened externally, inside, I was transformed from the kingdom of darkness into the kingdom of light as a new creature in Christ.[13] I poured myself into church activities and tried to do all of the right things, not understanding that I could never do the right things. Christ could do them through me, but I would never choose wisely until I allowed Him to show me who He is and who I am in Him.[14] He has commanded us to love Him first and others as we love ourselves. THAT was hard for me until I discovered that, in Christ, we are being made the righteousness of God![15] His ways are indeed higher than ours and better too.

On one church visitation, some of my friends wanted to visit a soldier they knew who was on leave from Vietnam. Meeting him that evening, I declared, "I am going to marry him." We dated for three weeks while he was home until he returned to Vietnam for another nine months. Just two weeks after my high school graduation and ten days after his return, we married. He was, after all, settled in a career with the army, and I was desperate for love and direction. Two and a half years later, our son was born.

The nurses at Camp Kue Army Hospital in Okinawa, Japan, where I was admitted at 10:30 p.m., had sent my husband home at midnight, saying, I was not in labor. He was to pick me up the next morning. Our son, Lee, was born at 3:30 a.m. After much insistence by me, the nurses finally reached my husband, and he arrived sometime later. However, alone in a foreign country at twenty years old, a baby was not the only thing born that night.

Unforgiveness began to grow, and that single root of bitterness eventually brought devastation and destruction to our marriage.

The choice not to forgive my husband for leaving me alone and at the mercy of the hospital in a foreign country was an unconscious one, but unforgiveness left untended grows into bitterness. Whatever we sow, we reap. Every choice has a consequence. Choose good, and get blessing and life; or choose evil, and get cursing and death. We must guard our hearts![16]

With our marriage failing, my husband and I made our final decision together: the geographical cure. Living at the beach would certainly make our life better and fix the problem. We extended a long weekend into a job search that resulted in my accepting a position comparable to the one I held, and we moved to St. Simons Island. It was a small town, with cottages and a couple of small inns, but there were no chain hotels or major shopping. It was close to perfect as a place to raise children and a place to dream.

Working for an insurance and real estate agency put me in contact with a variety of people and opened my eyes to the "good life." When my husband came home a few months later and quit his second job since moving to the island, my heart turned to stone. That seed of unforgiveness sown at my son's birth five years earlier grew into full flower, and our divorce was finalized exactly two months before our eighth anniversary. Believing the lie that divorce is an unpardonable sin, I spent the next three years on a path of self-destruction that only added fuel to the lies of my accuser.[17]

I sought comfort in alcohol, men, and work, but not necessarily in that order. Being held accountable for the responsibility of motherhood is what God used to keep me from total self-devastation. My son, however, paid a dear price for my promiscuity by not having stability in our home.

When my roommate told me of a position with Sea Island Golf Club, I quickly applied and got the job. Working in the pro shop was perfect, as I love people, clothes, and the beach. One of the perks, at that time, was that employees got a key to the north end of Sea Island. The key opened a gate to miles of untouched beaches and marshes to explore, usually without seeing another human being! Except for the momentary comfort of men, that north end was where I found peace.

My unhealed heart did not make healthy choices. Predators know when you are wounded and weak, and each encounter adds to the hurt. For every rejection, another affirmation must be sought, and so goes the cycle. Then, in an attempt to stop the cycle, I again chose the geographic cure.

In considering the move to Atlanta, I researched areas of the city to live and work where a car was unnecessary. Packing all our belongings in a Ryder truck, my seven-year-old and I moved to the "land of opportunity."

Before leaving, I spent one afternoon armed with a big black trash bag for treasures and a brown grocery bag for trash and headed to the north end. It became evident that there was more trash than treasure, so I adjusted the bags accordingly. From the corner of my eye, I caught a glimpse of a shiny red can and thought that I would pick it up on the way back. Instead, I walked from the wet sand toward the soft sand of the dunes to pick up the can. Beside it, half hidden by the loose sand, was the most beautiful driftwood I have ever seen. I would have missed it! It was a picture of life: in this world, there will always be much more trash than treasure, but if we go out of our way to make it better for others, we will be rewarded.

Chapter 3

THE PRODIGAL IN EXILE

The year was 1980, and I was living with Annie Kate Green in the old Morningside neighborhood of Atlanta, Georgia. Divorced and caring for a young son, the lure of the city had drawn me from the quiet life of St. Simons Island.

Because I believed a lie, I felt God was angry with me and could never accept me. I had gone too far. He was like Daddy or the other men in my life to whom I looked for approval and acceptance, or so I thought. That lie following divorce led to three years of what I have now called "self-imposed exile" because, if I was going to hell anyway, I may as well live like it. That is another big lie!

Hurt people hurt people. We all have hurts, and we have all hurt others. How we respond to hurt matters for our future.

Our lives are built on choices, and their resulting consequences often take us on paths we would rather not travel. There is a way that seems right, but there is a way that *is* right. He is faithful and merciful, and His lovingkindness is eternal. His name is Jesus, and before the world was created, He accepted the guilt we deserve.[18] He is the Lamb slain before the world Who takes away the sin of the world. I knew Him as a Savior, but I felt unworthy to call Him Lord, unworthy of His great grace. Yet through my rebellion, sin, and addiction, He was there. He is why I am still alive. He knows the plans He has for you, too, and they are good.

We moved from Annie Kate's home after a year because "I was too social." (She was a jewel to put it so nicely.) But without a stable place to live, the roller-coaster ride really began! I moved in with friends, but it was always the same. I was not a good influence on their children or mine. Place to place, job to job, man to man—the last year of chasing my dreams in Atlanta had added forty pounds to my body and torment to my soul. I hated the life I was living but had no idea I could find my way back to a normal life.

Working as a receptionist for a video production company, my son and I were living in the back of the studio. That is the closest to normal we got. A minor traffic accident brought me to the truth: We were homeless. I was a terrible mother who was not providing for her son!

My visions of grandeur had turned sour, and we were now sleeping in the car. It was then that I swallowed my pride and moved back to Dublin.

At the end of our will is One waiting with arms open wide to embrace, restore, and lead us. He knows our thoughts before we think of them, our secret sins, and our deepest fears, and still, He loves us.[19] He is for us.

Chapter 4

GOING HOME

Returning to Dublin, Georgia, where most of my family remained, was a humbling experience, especially when the only place for us to live was the old farmhouse where my grandparents had raised their family. The farm was to be sold and the house demolished, but we could live there rent-free in the interim.

Because it had been left fully furnished and now stood bulging with extra furniture and boxes stored from several generations, my challenge was to get one bedroom functional. The kitchen and bathroom were also made usable within the first week, but we literally walked a cleared pathway through boxes from room to room. It was worth the effort because being there was like coming to a place of safety. Memories of summers at my grandmother's house, Christmases spent with family in this place, and then my high school years when my family actually lived there all brought comfort to my weary and worn heart.

Finding a job, settling my son in school, and digging through years of memorabilia kept me occupied and interested for a season. Securing the finances to move the house to newly acquired land while arranging house movers and contractors kept me too busy to think about men, but only for a while.

Returning to the church that my mother had grown up in was easy because I myself had attended during high school. Many of the people knew me, loved me unconditionally, and welcomed me back.

Familiarity brought comfort as we settled into the routine of work, school, church, and renovating the house.

Church friends and work friends wanted to "fix me up" with their friends, and I did go out a couple of times. However, most of my free time was spent on the house project. But I was still desperate for affirmation and affection, so it was not long before I was in a relationship with one of the contractors. I was living a double life. Wanting to be free from the cycle of broken relationships, I began promising myself that this time would be different. But after using sex as a power tool for several years, the spirit may be willing, but the flesh is weak.[20] I fought the sexual addiction battle for years, and it is truly by God's grace that I am alive, well, and free today.

The longer we run from the truth, the harder it gets to find our way back. The longer we try to fill our lives with things other than God, the longer we live double-minded. Being double-minded is not only unstable, but it is also unhealthy. This often shows up in physical and/or mental illness. There is a way that seems right, but there is a right way.[21]

Light from a window will flood into the darkness when the curtains are opened, rather than the darkness flooding into the room. This is because light dispels darkness. Truth dispels lies. The enemy is called the accuser of the brethren, the father of lies, and the ruler of darkness. This is why turning to the light and walking in truth will make your way easier.

When the lies come, speak God's word, for it is truth. Allow Christ to shine in you, and He will transform you from the kingdom of darkness to His marvelous kingdom of light.

Chapter 5

RESTORATION BEGINS

Tackling the job of moving and restoring a house on a shoestring budget was my challenge. I found a part-time job quickly and devoted most of my time to the project. Climbing on the roof to remove the four chimneys was nothing compared to climbing down! Even Lee worked to relay brick up and out of the fireplaces. We enlisted a lot of help, but the black smutty work was reserved for us. The majority of bricks were salvaged to use at the new site.

During the month in preparation for the actual house moving, we sorted through the boxes in the house. Much was trash, which was put in the construction dumpster. The memorabilia were sorted by "owner" and each full box put in a specific corner. As the clutter began to diminish, I felt lighter inside too! The physical labor was helping remove some of the weight, but more importantly, my mind was being cleared of much of the fog.

I felt this, too, with clearing the new land. Tangled brush was cleared, trees removed, and a lot cleared for the house, which was brought in two pieces. The choice to remove the roof to reduce costs seemed like a good idea, but heavy rains during the first two weeks after it was moved actually caused more work. That lesson was not lost in my heart. One step forward, two steps back seemed to be a pattern that I desperately wanted to break.

Lee and I moved in with Mom while the house was being moved, but as soon as the roof was rebuilt, we were back in the old house. The plastic placed on the roof to protect the contents (four generations worth!) had not withheld the heavy winds and rain. This time of cleaning revealed that much of the memorabilia was ruined, but many furnishings were salvageable. We hauled trash and scrubbed walls for weeks before we could even begin the restoration process.

After three years of hard work, the house was finally livable, and though my body was tired, my mind was clearer. Taking something that others thought should be destroyed and giving it a new purpose is God's specialty. He uses the foolish things of the world to confound the wise. He never despises a broken, contrite heart that cries out to Him.[22] I know this from experience. He took me from the pit and set my feet on a rock[23].

They called Jesus a winebibber, glutton, and friend of sinners because He hung out with those who drank, ate, and sinned! But He came not to participate in sin but so that those in darkness might be transformed into the kingdom of light. He told the woman caught in adultery to go and sin no more. He will meet you where you are if you call to Him. Do not believe the lie that you have gone too far, done too much, or backslidden too many times. God's grace is sufficient. He is slow to anger and abounding in love. Yes, He is righteous and holy, but His mercy is new every day, and He is longing for His children to believe in Him and the One He sent: Jesus Christ—the way, the truth, and life.[24]

Chapter 6

SEARCH FOR SIGNIFICANCE

Being very involved in church was uncomfortable when I was in addiction, so I chose to become active in community affairs—in more ways than one, unfortunately. Dublin has long been a great community with many organizations that are ready to accept workers. Character standards are not always so high as those in church!

Several opportunities for job advancement were presented, though some of them offered more than even I was willing to accept. Those encounters made me realize I had to get help. But trying to find someone I could trust to help rather than hurt made me give up and take the geographic cure, again.

I found a new start in a new community. Because the position of executive director of the convention and visitors bureau demanded most of my time as I was learning a new community, I quickly found a church home, eager to "do it right" this time. When a weekend revival was held over to Monday night, I was in a dilemma. The governor's conference on tourism started Tuesday morning, and I was presenting at an early session that morning. The plan had been to join my board of directors at the capitol on Monday afternoon for the legislative dinner hosted by our community that night.

After wrestling with God most of the night, I knew that if I returned to Atlanta for a "wine and dine," I would fall back into the same patterns of destruction that come with addiction. Instead, I chose to drive to Atlanta early Tuesday morning so I could attend revival and still do my presentation at the conference. The decision could cost me my job, but though disappointed, the board respected my decision.

Shortly thereafter, two men from church expressed an interest in going out with me: one, a surgeon whose goal was to become a medical missionary, and the other, a business owner. I chose the business owner because, though he was successful, he was also recovering alcoholic. I felt unworthy to date a doctor who wanted to be a missionary! (Though I had felt God wanted me to be a missionary since age eighteen.)

We dated for a short time and then married. The travel involved in my job began to threaten the marriage, so again, I was at a crossroads—values over position. I left the job and began working with my husband. Both the business and the marriage seemed to flourish, and I was living the dream, or so it seemed.

The enemy of our souls hates God with such passion that he will stop at nothing to destroy one of His image bearers.[25] Anything unconfessed is still hidden in darkness, and that is the enemy's domain. When we confess our sins, Christ can shine a light on them and in us, which dispels darkness. The reason twelve-step groups are so popular is that you confess your sins without judgment, and then others help bear your burden, encouraging you to stay clean, sober, and/or straight. The church of the living God must do the same—coming alongside those who fall short of the glory of God because we remember where we came from! There is none righteous without Christ.

Chapter 7

BETRAYAL

We did everything together—building houses, traveling, working, and playing. However, he began to explore the supernatural, eventually questioning the very word of God. My faith was strong, and surely, he would come again to the truth. I was so afraid of another divorce that even his searching for the "deeper things of God" was not enough for me to leave.

Eight years after saying "I do," my husband declared he wanted to share our marriage bed with another woman, and my heart was pulverized. This was my second marriage, and we had met in a prayer group at church! Certainly, this could not be happening again. But it was. For months, I was unable to eat as he announced that he wanted to be married to me for one week, with "her" for one week, and free for two weeks each month.

After a year of back and forth, he filed for divorce, and I was devastated again.

Emaciated, depressed, and suicidal, I returned to Dublin and to the church my mom still attended, where I could be surrounded by the unconditional love of God through His people. A group of ladies were forming a prayer group, so I joined. God used those ladies to restore my life. They encouraged me, loved me, and laughed and cried with me, but they would not let me stay in self-pity. Cami, Frances, Judy, and Kathy (the four ladies who were the core of that group) will always be my heroes, for God used them to literally save my life. From them, I learned to do what is before you, to give everything to God, to love without strings, and to live every day as if it were the last day on earth.

Chapter 8

STRIKE THREE

However, I was a slow learner. During this time of devastation, a young man at church began showing me attention and stirring in me those desires that had once ruled my life. Against the counsel of my friends, we married. Almost immediately, he became physically abusive, but I was too proud to admit another mistake, so I tried to pretend he was going to change.

"What did I do to deserve this?" The question popped into my mind as I lay cowering on the floor, maneuvering to keep the phone from hitting my face and head as my enraged husband was uncontrollably beating me with anything he could put his hands on.

It was not the first time. I always said, "If a man hits me once, he won't get a second chance!" But I was wounded, and my unhealed heart drove me to make unhealthy choices. Instead of allowing God to be my husband after a horrific divorce, I was swept off my feet by this man, and within a few months, we married. He was addicted to pain pills, but I was addicted to him and hopelessly codependent!

After his first binge of alcohol, drugs, and abuse, he spent time in jail. However, while he sat in jail, I got news that my former husband died unexpectedly. My emotions were raw, and the pain of past hurts clouded my thoughts. I accepted his apology and took him back.

That is how I found myself rolling on the floor that night when I heard God's voice, say, "There is nothing you could ever do that would deserve this." I was lying there, taking the abuse, when a strange peace came over me. I relaxed and quit struggling, and immediately, he began apologizing and trying to make amends. By the grace of God, he fell asleep as he began to seduce me, and I was able to get safely away. I insisted he get help, and he entered a drug rehabilitation program. I got serious about my codependency issues, but the idea of another divorce was more than I could bear, so when he was released, he moved back in.

By the grace of God and the help of friends who helped me set up a code, they checked on me often and knew that if I said a certain innocent-sounding phrase, they were to send the police immediately. One Sunday morning, he was angry, and he threw me around, but I landed on the bed, so he grabbed my ankles and dragged me to the floor. I told him he better let me call my friends because if I was not at church as usual, they would come and check on me. It must have made sense to him because he let me call them, and I told them I was not going to make church. Of course, I added the code phrase, and soon the police were hauling him to jail again. Now completely broken, I got a restraining order and filed for divorce.

Addiction is an all-consuming demon. It may seem to start gradually, but when it is full-blown, it leads you to do things you would never do. No one suffering from addiction wants to lie, steal, murder, deceive, or self-destruct, but that is the end result of addiction of any kind.[26]

The only answer to addiction is a relationship with Jesus Christ, Who came to set us free. God, Creator of the universe and all that it contains, because of His great love for His image bearers, became flesh to live as a human.

In the beginning was the Word, and the Word was with God, and the Word was God.[27] In Him was life, and the life was the light of men. Jesus Christ is the Word made flesh! God in human form. In Him, we can have life and live abundantly. There is no chain He cannot break, no shame He cannot take, no hurt He cannot heal, and no pain He cannot feel. He became our sin, brokenness, shame, guilt, and misery. Come, be washed in the blood of the Lamb and drink of the river of life. You will discover that He is more than enough to satisfy every longing and fill every need.

Chapter 9

HOPE RESTORED

How does healing begin? Healing only comes through a relationship with Jesus Christ, Who became sin so we could be made the righteousness of God in Him.

With three failed marriages, there was no way I wanted another man in my life. Instead, I let my *true love* teach me what love is and who I am. The Word of God became my life. Through it, God revealed how my childhood hurt manifested into a warped perception of myself and God, which led to dysfunction. Poor choices are the result of wrong information. In my mind, I was damaged because of sexual abuse, so I had to earn approval from men. But sexuality is a gift from God, and when used outside of the boundaries He created (a committed, monogamous, and lifelong marriage), it can never be satisfied. (The sexual urge, once perverted in an individual, will make that person desire more, different, better. It is addictive.) The good news is that Jesus Christ became our sin so we could be made the righteousness of God. We do not have to stay in sexual perversion!

First, we must recognize that we are desperately lost in sin without Christ, and we need a way of escape. Jesus is the way! When we get to the end of our will, God will always meet us there if we call on Him. If you have never asked Jesus Christ to come into your heart because you thought you had to get your act together first, let me tell you from experience: *You will never get your act together without Jesus*

Christ. It is God Who begins the work and completes it.[28] Our duty is to BELIEVE Him, not just believe *in* Him. Even devils believe in Jesus and tremble.

The Word of God states, "You shall love the Lord your God with all your heart, with all your soul, and with all your mind This is the first and great commandment. And the second is like it: You shall love your neighbor as yourself." The Holy Spirit burned this in my heart. "That is what we do, and that is the problem."

After an hour of travail, all I could do was weep for myself and the millions of others who have allowed the lies of the enemy, whether they came from our own choices or the choices of others, to rob us of our identity. Each of us was created in the image of the Most High GOD. Each of us is special, uniquely gifted for such a time as this. Within each of us is the promise of God waiting for us to turn from self, be washed in the blood of Jesus Christ, and be filled with His Holy Spirit as new creatures in Christ. It is a mystery, but it is proven by the fact that this unplanned pregnancy resulted in a young girl who, though abused by herself and others, can now stand before God Himself, spotless and without blame in love.

Chapter 10

HEALING THE HURT

Having found the perfect husband in God, I no longer needed to look for a man.[29] Being with friends at parties or singles gatherings with the church was enough of a social outlet. Prayer and Bible study dominated most of my waking hours. Working one or two days a week meant most of my time was spent in what I call God's "intensive care unit." We spent hours together, and I began to understand how my poor choices were often the result of wounds that were not healed but buried.

One by one, the events and people surrounding these wounds were dragged out of the closet and into the light. I had a choice. I could acknowledge it, accept responsibility for it, and allow God to shine His light on it, or I could refuse, and it would be hidden again. Each time, as the light shone, darkness was dispelled! Eighteen months to heal forty-six years of hurt is amazing because I was stubborn and rebellious for much of my life. Like the stiff-necked Israelites, it took me a long time to truly learn lessons.

The gift of God is without repentance, which means it cannot be changed. Before the world began, God knew you and the choices you would make, but He loves you anyway and is calling to you now, saying, "You are my beloved. Accept My gift of love and let Me heal your hurt and transform your life. I know the plans I have for you, and they are for good, not evil." If you were betrayed by your earthly father or never knew your biological father, it may seem impossible to trust that God is your Father and that He loves you without conditions. ·

If you drag His name through the mud, He loves you. If you give Him praise every day, He loves you. His love is so much higher than our minds can comprehend, but it is such a comfort to know that nothing can ever separate us from His love in Christ.[30] He created us to love Him and be loved by Him, just as surely as He created us to have love here on earth. The problem is that we try to fulfill the longing for love, which can only be filled by believing Jesus Christ PAID IN FULL the sin debt we have, with people, places, and things. Nothing will ever satisfy the longing of your heart until you realize you were created by God Himself to be loved by Him.

Chapter 11

UNEXPECTED JOY

One day, as I turned the corner to my house, I looked in desperation at the neglected lawn and said, "God, I need a husband to help with this grass." He must have chuckled because, within weeks, a friend asked me out. Bill was a photographer, so I had helped him as he photographed weddings. Because I decorated for weddings, he had helped me with that too. But dating was something I feared.

Having a man treat me to a nice evening out meant I was obligated to him. Going to dinner turned into going to bed. So I canceled the date and told him I wanted to remain friends. He was not amused and said that our friendship was too close, and he wanted our relationship to build to marriage. I was shocked. Sure, we had known each other for a couple of years and for the previous six months we had spent a lot of time together, talking daily on the phone for months, but in my mind, he was a great guy and a wonderful friend, nothing more. So when he told me I had a choice: go forward in the relationship or end it, I said goodbye.

Even as I hung up the phone, I felt empty, but I shrugged it off until later that evening. My pride said I did not need a man, and certainly not one shorter than me, but my heart was telling me another story. As his friend, I had learned that Bill was dependable, helpful, wise, funny, and walking out His faith in Christ like no one I had ever seen. I was comfortable with him and can be myself when we were together without having to entertain or impress him. But my past experiences proved I did not have the best judgment, especially when it came to men, so I balked.

As I held a wooden spoon Bill had carved and given me, I cried uncontrollably and asked God what was going on. As we argued, God reminded me that my heart's desire was to see with His eyes and love with His heart. So when He asked me the simple question, "Are you going to walk it or just talk it?" that hurt! All weekend, I wrestled with God about Bill and ultimately admitted that I did love him and asked both God and him to forgive me.

We married just two months later, and Bill has proven himself to be a better man than I ever imagined he could be. Because of God putting Bill in my life, I am a better person and challenged to be even better every day.

Bill's only rule when we married was simple but effective: If we argue, we have to remove our clothes and go to the bedroom.

So whenever tempers start to flare, one of us asks if we are arguing, and we both remember the rules. Usually, that is all it takes to make us stop, drop it, and laugh because it is some silly difference of opinion. However, even if it is something important we disagree about, remembering that if we argue, we get naked changes the mood, and we are no longer angry and defensive, but we are able to discuss the matter. We have learned how to disagree without being disagreeable, which is an art in itself and a gift from God!

Chapter 12

LIVING IN LOVE

Where does love begin? Love begins in God.

In the beginning, Creator God spoke all things into existence, but He reached into the dirt with His own hands and created man in His own image. Then He breathed life into man.[31]

In the perfection of creation, man and woman were free to enjoy each other and everything over which they had dominion. There was one rule, but there was no shame, guilt, or pain. Perfect love ruled supreme, until, through a single act of disobedience, sin entered the world. Yet God, in His infinite mercy, offered the first blood sacrifice as He clothed Adam and Eve and sent them away from Paradise.

I believe God is calling us back to the freedom of paradise and has made the way for us to live in peace, walk in authority, and exercise dominion over everything on earth. Christ came to destroy the works of the devil.[32] He completed the work when He fulfilled the law of sin and death. He paid the debt. It is finished. The power of the resurrection is available to us as it was to Jesus Christ. We can come out of the tomb, put off the graveclothes, and walk in liberty if we believe in the Lord Jesus Christ.

God has given all authority to Jesus and, through Him, to us. As long as we continue to think we have to *do* something to get to God, we are trapped. God is everywhere, all-powerful, and He knows everything. We are human beings, not human doings. God asks us to believe in Him and His Son, Jesus. If we believe *in* Him, we have to begin to *believe* Him. Faith is not seeing.[33] It is confidence that the unseen is real. And faith comes by hearing the Word of God.[34]

John 1:1 says that God is His Word. There is much debate about how literal is God's Word. I do not worship the book called the Bible, but I worship the Lord God Almighty. And that same God who I know through faith in Jesus Christ is the Word. In the beginning was the Word, and the Word was with God, and the Word was God. To know God is to know His Word, and as I read it every day, I am changed. It gives me guidance, comfort, hope, and strength.

"It feels like I studied my lines and knew my part perfectly, but when the curtain went up, I was in the wrong play." Spoken casually in the midst of self-imposed exile, these words would haunt me every time there was a crisis in my life. As I have pondered them through the years, I have come to realize that I was absolutely correct. I was created for much more. Jesus Christ came that we might have life and have it abundantly.

Let me invite you into new life by recognizing that no one comes to God except the Spirit of God draws Him, and that way is through faith in the work of Jesus Christ. He not only died for your sin, but He also conquered death with His resurrection and is now making intercession for you at the right hand of God the Father.[35] There is no formula, so let your heart cry out to the One Who is Perfect Freedom, asking Jesus to forgive you and allow His Holy Spirit, Christ in you, to help change you.[36] Father is willing to move heaven and earth on behalf of those who will trust in the finished work of His Son, Jesus. He has done it for me, and He will do it for you.

We are saved by the grace of God through our faith in Christ Jesus, acknowledging Him as Savior and allowing Him to assume lordship of our lives. He will do exceedingly abundantly above all you can ask or think if you will deny your flesh, take up your cross, and follow Him. Only one person did this perfectly, and that person is the incarnate God, our Lord Jesus Christ. But He lives in us through the Holy Spirit, the Spirit of Truth, the helper He promised that Father would send when He returned to glory with His Father.

I challenge you to try calling on Jesus Christ and speaking His name out loud every time you are tempted, angry, hurt, or confused. Ask Him to open your eyes and heart and to reveal Himself to you. He promises that as we draw near to Him, seeking Him with all our hearts, He will manifest Himself to us. His ways are higher than ours, and His plans are better. He does work ALL things together for good for those who love Him and are called according to His purpose.[37]

If He can take an abused and confused little girl from fear and unworthiness to abundant life, there is nothing He cannot do for you too. For many years, He has allowed me to minister to women, placing me full-time in leadership of a local mission to women. Anything good that has been accomplished through ABC Women's Clinic for those twenty years has totally been His doing, and I am humbled to be His slave, willing and obedient to my Master's command. There is joy unspeakable, peace beyond understanding, and love immeasurable in the center of God's will. I pray you will seek for yourself all that He is and all that He has for you.

Believe

Endnotes

1. Genesis 3:8–10
2. Proverbs 22:15
3. Deuteronomy 30:15–20
4. Galatians 6:7–8
5. Jeremiah 31:3
6. Ephesians 1:4–10
7. Ephesians 1 13–14
8. Jeremiah 29:11
9. Psalms 139:16
10. Genesis 2:18–25
11. 1 John 4:7–10
12. Romans 3:23, Romans 6:23, Romans 10:9–10
13. 2 Peter 2:9
14. John 14:6
15. 2 Corinthians 5:21
16. Proverbs 4:23
17. 1 Peter 5:8
18. John 1:29, Revelation 5:6
19. Psalms 139:1–3
20. Romans 7:14–25, Matthew 26:40–41
21. Proverbs 14:12
22. Psalm 51:17
23. Psalm 40:2
24. John 14:6
25. .1 Peter 5:8
26. Romans 1:28–32
27. John 1:1–5
28. Philippians 1:6
29. Isaiah 54:4–10
30. Romans 8:35–39
31. Genesis 2:7
32. 1 John 3:8
33. Hebrews 11:1
34. Romans 10:17

35 Romans 8:34, Hebrews 7:25, 1 John 2:1
36 Colossians 1:27
37 Romans 8:28

About the Author

Rebecca began her career as a lifeguard, transitioned through secretary and bookkeeper to public relations, and then thought her fifteen-year-old decorating business would be where she would stay.

However, God had other plans and called her into pro-life ministry, from which she retired after twenty years. She is married to William, and together, they have two children, six grandchildren, and four great-granddaughters under the age of four!

Rebecca and William are actively involved at Connection Church Dublin, near where they reside, and continue to connect people to a growing relationship with Jesus Christ.